CELEBRATING
50 YEARS
Texas A&M University Press
publishing since 1974

To Del Rio, TX.
-Lisa Johansson

Blindcat and Tadpole

Lisa Johansson

Illustrated by Bianka Santillan

Will and Pamela Nelson Harte Series on Water and the Environment
Sponsored by

The Meadows Center for Water and the Environment
TEXAS STATE UNIVERSITY

Andrew Sansom, General Editor

Texas A&M University Press   College Station

Tadpole turned sixty days old. He swam in the shallow waters of *la poza del sol*. The sun was bright, and he was surrounded by his brothers and sisters. They bumped up against one another as they fed on the soft algae floating between them.

He knew he had to stay near his siblings so he would not be eaten by a fish. He was eager for his *metamorphosis,* a change that would help him explore the world beyond the water's edge.

Only some creatures get to experience such a big change. Tadpole felt proud to be an *amphibian.*

He practiced swimming faster and faster every day. He wished the days would hurry up so he could move out of the crowded pond.

The blazing sun warmed the water, and *la poza del sol* seemed to be shrinking. Tadpole and his siblings were growing, and soon they would run out of swimming space. If only his legs would grow quicker!

On Tadpole's ninetieth day in the pool, he noticed clouds filling the sky and covering the sun.

The water grew darker and cooler. Tadpole watched the wind ripple across the surface, and a shiver raced down his tail.

Drip.

Drop.

The sky opened, and heavy rain fell.

The water became blurry as it sloshed back and forth, and Tadpole could hardly see his brothers and sisters. Light flashed across the sky with a loud clap. Suddenly, a current pulled him backwards. He struggled to swim forward, but the rushing water was too powerful.

Tadpole was being swept away in a *flash flood.* The water tossed him in every direction, and the ground opened up beneath him. He crashed into a rock and tumbled into a deep sinkhole.

Tadpole splashed into a pool of water at the bottom of the hole. Everything was dark and silent.

He blinked and strained to see a faint glimmer of light ahead. As he swam toward it, Tadpole noticed an object drifting in and out of the shimmering beams of light. It was a fish!

Its body was pale with pinkish, *translucent* skin. Glints of light passed through its delicate fins as they waved like thin silk fans in the dark water.

Tadpole tried to sneak away, but the gentle current pushed the sleeping fish into him. Tadpole froze in fear.

The fish startled and woke with an odd grunt. It swung its mouth back and forth like it was tasting the water, and Tadpole backed against the wall. Surely it was going to eat him!

How could Tadpole swim away? His tail bumped against the cave walls, and he could barely see in front of him. He tried to calm himself by imagining his siblings next to him as the strange sounds drew closer.

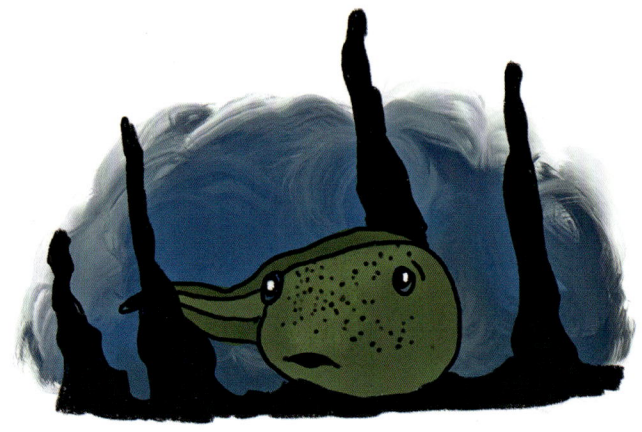

Finally, the fish fell silent. Then a snout with long whiskers emerged from the murky water, and Tadpole heard a low, quiet voice ask, "Are you a tadpole? What are you doing down here?"

Tadpole stammered, "Y-y-yes, I am a t-tadpole. Who are you?"

"I am Blindcat. I am a cave-dwelling catfish, specifically a Mexican blindcat, of the genus *Prietella*." His voice rose and fell in a slow cadence. "What are you doing at the entrance to my cave?"

The fish's *barbels* gracefully curled back and forth, dancing through the water. Tadpole saw Blindcat had no eyes at all!

"I don't know how I got here," Tadpole whimpered. "I want to go back to *la poza del sol*."

Blindcat's whiskers arched back toward his *pectoral fins*. "I have never been to *la poza del sol*. . . You are in my home, *las cuevas mágicas*. My home is part of a *karst aquifer* that stretches from Coahuila to *Tejas*. Every season, every day, it changes. That is why they are called magic caves."

Tadpole's face brightened. "If the caves are magic, can I use magic to get out?"

Blindcat chuckled. "No, but the magic can guide you." He paused for a moment, then continued, "I could help you reach your home, but I am tired from my feast at the bottom of the sinkhole. Fresh rain always brings food from the surface."

"How long have you lived here?" Tadpole peered at Blindcat in the dim light.

"This is my ninetieth season," Blindcat said.

"Before I fell, I turned ninety days old." Tadpole's voice cracked, "I am supposed to go through metamorphosis and grow legs soon."

"You are in a hurry, and I am ready for my rest," Blindcat yawned. Tadpole could smell the food in the back of his large mouth. "I am so full. . . I need a nap." He yawned again and turned back toward the shadows.

"Wait!" Tadpole darted after the fish. "Will you please help me? I can barely see, and I cannot get out the same way I came in."

Blindcat flicked his tail impatiently. He just wanted to drift back to his favorite rock and sleep.

Tadpole worried that Blindcat would leave him alone, but then the fish went still.

"You remind me of my friend, Texen," Blindcat spoke into the gloom. "He was an isopod, *Cirolanides texensis*. When we were young, we chased each other through the passages of these caves. Every twist and turn of *las cuevas mágicas* revealed a new adventure for us.

"I miss my old friend," Blindcat grinned and turned back to Tadpole. "I will help you. But the path to the surface is dangerous."

"How can you lead me through the danger if you cannot see?" Tadpole glanced again at Blindcat's eyeless face.

Blindcat replied, "I sense with my whiskers and fins. I detect the movement and pressure of the water across my *lateral lines*. I feel the noises and taste the scents in the cave. You can see if you use your senses, too.

"Come. I will take you to a secret portal," Blindcat offered, "but I cannot get too close. Some of my friends have never returned from there."

Blindcat and Tadpole set off on their journey. The blind fish swam ahead and hummed a quiet song so the young amphibian could follow him.

Tadpole strained to see, but it was completely black. As they made their way into total darkness, Tadpole struggled to use his other senses the way Blindcat had described.

As they swam, Tadpole noticed a current of cool water slide past him. Then he realized Blindcat's humming did not echo, as if the cave walls were truly magic and swallowed the sound. With his other senses now on full alert, Tadpole became more aware of the *cave formations*, and he felt the passageways growing narrower!

Blindcat stopped abruptly, making Tadpole bump into him.

"This is my home," said Blindcat. "Can you feel it?

"It is always calm and quiet here. The limestone protects me. Go ahead, explore while I will rest." With that, Blindcat fell silent.

Tadpole hesitantly moved in each direction, careful to not disturb Blindcat's sleep. The cave formations pressed close and reminded him of the crowded pond with his brothers and sisters. Tadpole felt safe. Perhaps Blindcat's home was like his own.

After some time, Blindcat stirred and announced, "I am ready to take you the rest of the way."

They swam together in a steady rhythm, and Tadpole began humming along with Blindcat.

Eventually, Blindcat slowed down and stopped humming. Tadpole could sense the tension in the fish's movements.

"We have reached the most dangerous part of our journey. My mother warned me to stay away from this tunnel," Blindcat said with alarm in his voice. "The water keeps changing. We don't understand why, but it burns our skin, smells foul, and hurts our *ecosystem*."

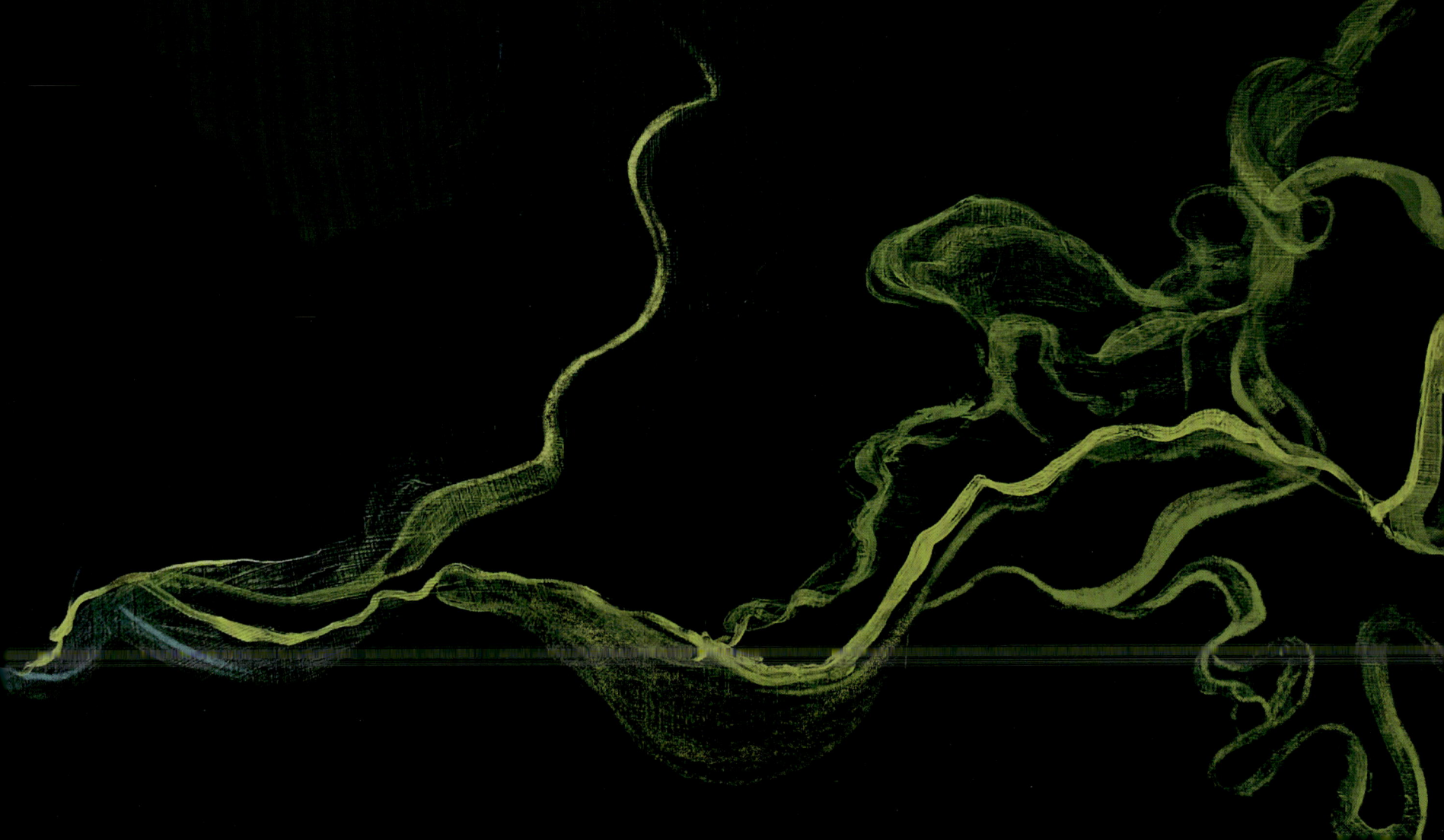

Blindcat's voice dropped to an urgent whisper, "We must swim through as fast as possible. Do not swallow this water. Follow me!"

Tadpole took one last gulp and scurried behind Blindcat. The water burned his eyes and *spiracles*. He could feel Blindcat swimming ahead of him, his fins carving through the thick water.

When they made it across, they took a moment to fill their mouths with fresh water, then the pair resumed their journey through the magic caves.

After a long straightaway, Blindcat came to a halt again. "Do you hear it?"

Tadpole heard a sound like the wind.

"Are you ready to go back to the surface?" asked Blindcat.

Tadpole realized he was very tired. "How will I swim to the surface?"

Blindcat laughed, "This is an *artesian spring!* Water is pushed upward by the pressure in the surrounding rocks. If you get close enough, the current will carry you back to the surface!"

Tadpole remembered being swept away by the current in *la poza del sol* and twitched his tail anxiously. Blindcat explained, "Every aquifer has entrances and exits. Freshwater constantly filters in and out. Its magic brings in food, carves the walls, and creates my home. The flash flood that brought you here and this artesian spring are part of the magic."

Blindcat is wise, Tadpole thought as he peered into the dark. *Ninety seasons must be much longer than ninety days.*

Tadpole turned toward Blindcat's voice once more. "Will the artesian spring take me back to *la poza del sol*?"

"No." Blindcat said gently. "It leads to a new place. When you make it to the surface, you will be on your own, but you will be safe."

Tadpole remained silent.

"Most creatures don't know about *las cuevas mágicas*. The caves connect many bodies of water. Did you want to spend your whole life in *la poza del sol*?" asked Blindcat.

"I knew I wasn't going to stay there forever," Tadpole confessed, "but I am scared of the change."

Blindcat reassured him, "You have gotten stronger and grown on our journey. You must go before you are too big to fit through the spring."

Tadpole leaned into Blindcat. He was grateful for his help. "Will you come with me? Don't you want to see the surface?"

"Heavens, no! What could there possibly be to see when I already live in a world of magic?" Blindcat gently nudged Tadpole toward the spring. "Now go, my friend."

Tadpole backed away from Blindcat. The current caught him and propelled him upward faster and faster. He burst out of the small tunnel into a pool of shallow water!

Tadpole squinted in the bright sunlight sparkling on the water's surface. When his eyes adjusted, he saw plants, small fish, and even some other tadpoles. There were long stems and green leaves all around.

The artesian spring had carried him to an entirely new home!

Tadpole pushed effortlessly through the water with his budding hind legs. He nibbled on the new plants and basked in the sun's warmth. He was delighted to find this pond so different from *la poza del sol* yet so familiar.

Tadpole swam to the edge of the weeds and looked back at the small hole at the bottom of the pond. Fresh water swelled up from below and drifted toward Tadpole. He relaxed as the cool water and blades of grass at the water's edge pressed against him like the walls of Blindcat's home.

Tadpole drifted through the pond and felt *las cuevas mágicas*.

Glossary

amphibian: A type of cold-blooded vertebrate that lives in water and on land. Amphibians, like a frog or salamander, begin their lives as larvae with gills and undergo a complex change to become land-dwelling animals that have lungs and breathe air.

artesian spring: Water forced to the surface due to pressure underground.

barbels: Whiskers used to help catfish find food in water with poor visibility. The barbels have taste receptors to determine if something is a source of food or danger.

cave formations: Caves are formed by the dissolution (breaking down) of limestone. Rain droplets pick up carbon dioxide from the air and form small amounts of carbonic acid. As the acidic rain moves through rock (calcium carbonate), the slightly acidic rain water breaks it apart, forming caves and interesting cave features such as stalagmites, stalactites, columns, drapery, or tunnels.

***Cirolanides texensis*:** A cave-dwelling isopod. Isopods are invertebrates (no backbone).

ecosystem: A biological community of interacting organisms and their physical environment.

flash flood: Heavy rainfall, usually from a large storm, that quickly produces large amounts of runoff water at the surface. Flash floods can carry debris, damage property, and destroy the lives of those in its path.

genus *Prietella*: In biology, living organisms are classified by their characteristics into broad groups, such as a family, and narrowed down into more specific groups called species. Genus is the level above species, where organisms share many characteristics but not all. The science of naming and classifying organisms is called taxonomy.

karst aquifer: Karst is a type of landscape containing porous rock (rock that contains holes like a sponge). In Northern Mexico and South Texas, this type of rock is limestone, or calcium carbonate. An aquifer is the water contained by rock under the surface. In a karst aquifer, underground water flows to the surface in fresh springs.

la poza del sol: The sunny pond, Spanish.

las cuevas mágicas: The magic caves, Spanish.

lateral lines: A sensory system used by fish to detect movement, vibration, and pressure changes in its aquatic environment. It is a series of pores that run along a fish's body. Each pore is connected to a nerve ending that relays information to the brain. Lateral lines are used by fish to navigate, locate prey, and avoid predators.

metamorphosis: A biological process where an animal undergoes a physical change in distinct phases, resulting in a new body structure through cell growth and differentiation. Tadpoles change quickly from egg to larva (tadpole) to an adult (frog).

pectoral fins: A wing-like body part of fish located behind the head. Pectoral fins are used to control the forward and side to side movement of fish.

spiracles: The openings on both sides of a tadpole that enable it to breathe underwater.

translucent: A characteristic that allows some light to pass through an object.

***Tejas*:** Texas, Spanish.

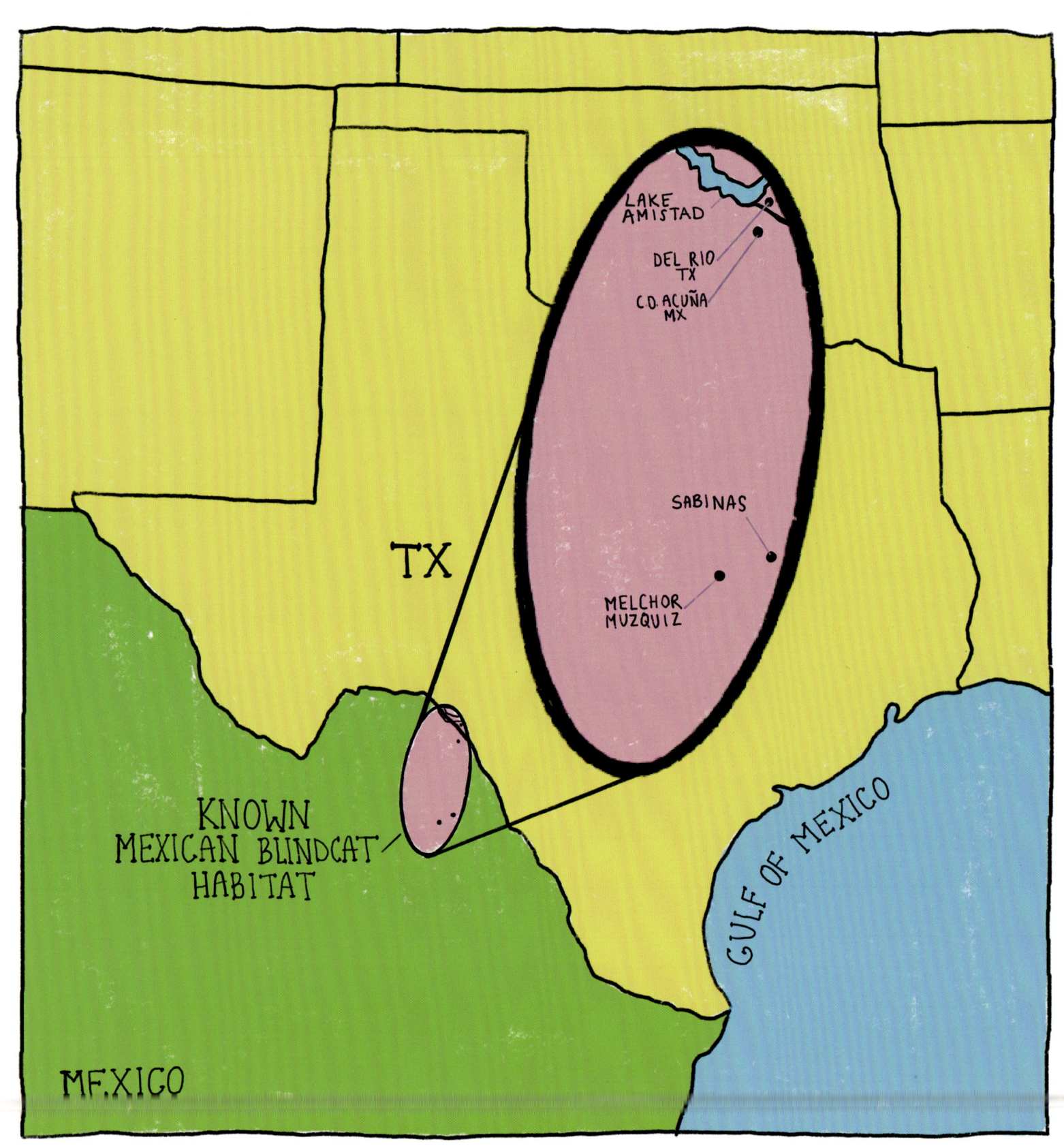

Biography

The Mexican blindcat, scientific name *Prietella phreatophila* [PRY-ah-tell-ah free-ah-TOE-fill-ah], is an endemic cave-dwelling catfish found only in Northern Mexico and the southern border of Texas near Coahuila. The blindcat grows to be three to four inches in length and is the top predator in its ecosystem! In Coahuila, Mexico, the blindcat is commonly called "el Bagre de Múzquiz" after the town, Múzquiz, where it is most frequently found.

Until 2016, the Mexican blindcat had only been seen in Mexico. The Amistad Reservoir (also called Lake Amistad) and the Rio Grande are internationally shared bodies of water on the United States-Mexico border. A team of cavers found Mexican blindcats on the northern side of the border, proving the aquifers must be connected *under* the border. An expert caver, Peter Sprouse, found the blindcat in a shallow cave at the edge of Lake Amistad. The species was already fully protected under the U.S. Endangered Species Act, so the Texas population of blindcats was immediately protected.

The species *Prietella phreatophila* is estimated to be up to thirty million years old! Scientists believe the Mexican blindcat is a descendant of surface catfish, of the genus *Ameiurus,* generally known as "bullhead catfish." Surface catfish are nocturnal and like to hide in caves and crevices. Perhaps some got trapped in caves during times of drought, or perhaps they preferred staying in small caves. Over many generations, the fish lost their sight. Losing their sight is estimated to conserve between five to fifteen percent of their total energy consumption. Many other cave species have evolved to be blind, such as the blind salamander, Mexican tetra, and blind shrimp.

The Mexican blindcat has no need for sight because its environment is completely dark. To navigate the underground passageways, blindcats use other sensory organs such as their lateral lines. They have an incredible olfactory (smell) system and sensitive barbels that help them find food. In the laboratory, blindcats eat anything fed to them.

Cave species rely on nutrients that come from the surface. During times of drought, water may not flow from the surface into their caves for weeks or months at a time. Cave ecosystems are low-energy environments, and food is scarce. Blindcats are experts at conserving energy and can go long stretches without eating. The longest documented period without food in the laboratory was forty-four months (three years, eight months)! In captivity, scientists observed the fish had long periods of inactivity. Sometimes the researchers thought the fish were dead, but they were just floating belly-up while resting! Scientists hypothesize blindcats could have a lifespan up to one hundred years.

Las cuevas mágicas are not really magic, but rather, the formations in the caves seem to magically change over time due to erosion and chemical reactions between rainwater and limestone (rocks). Millions of years ago, Northern Mexico and Texas were submerged in seawater. Over millions of years, Earth has experienced long periods of cold (ice ages) and warm (interglacials). During this time, land emerged in this area, leaving fossil remains and, eventually, karst topography and cave formations.

Although the Mexican blindcat has existed for millions of years, its greatest threat is habitat change from humans. As cities and industry near the border expand, the demand for freshwater rises. Blindcats are sensitive to changes in water chemistry. Agricultural wastes, like fertilizer and pesticides, can quickly run off into underground aquifers. Ranchers in Coahuila have shared stories about dumping lye (sodium hydroxide NaOH) into wells to disinfect it after an animal has fallen in the well. After the decontamination process, dead blindcats were found floating in the well. Other chemicals, like human hormones, may affect the blindcats' ability to reproduce. When researchers first transported blindcats to laboratories, many fish got infections and died. Although blindcats are well-adapted to live in their unique environment, they are not able to adjust to some of the changes taking place at the surface.

Anatomy of the Blindcat

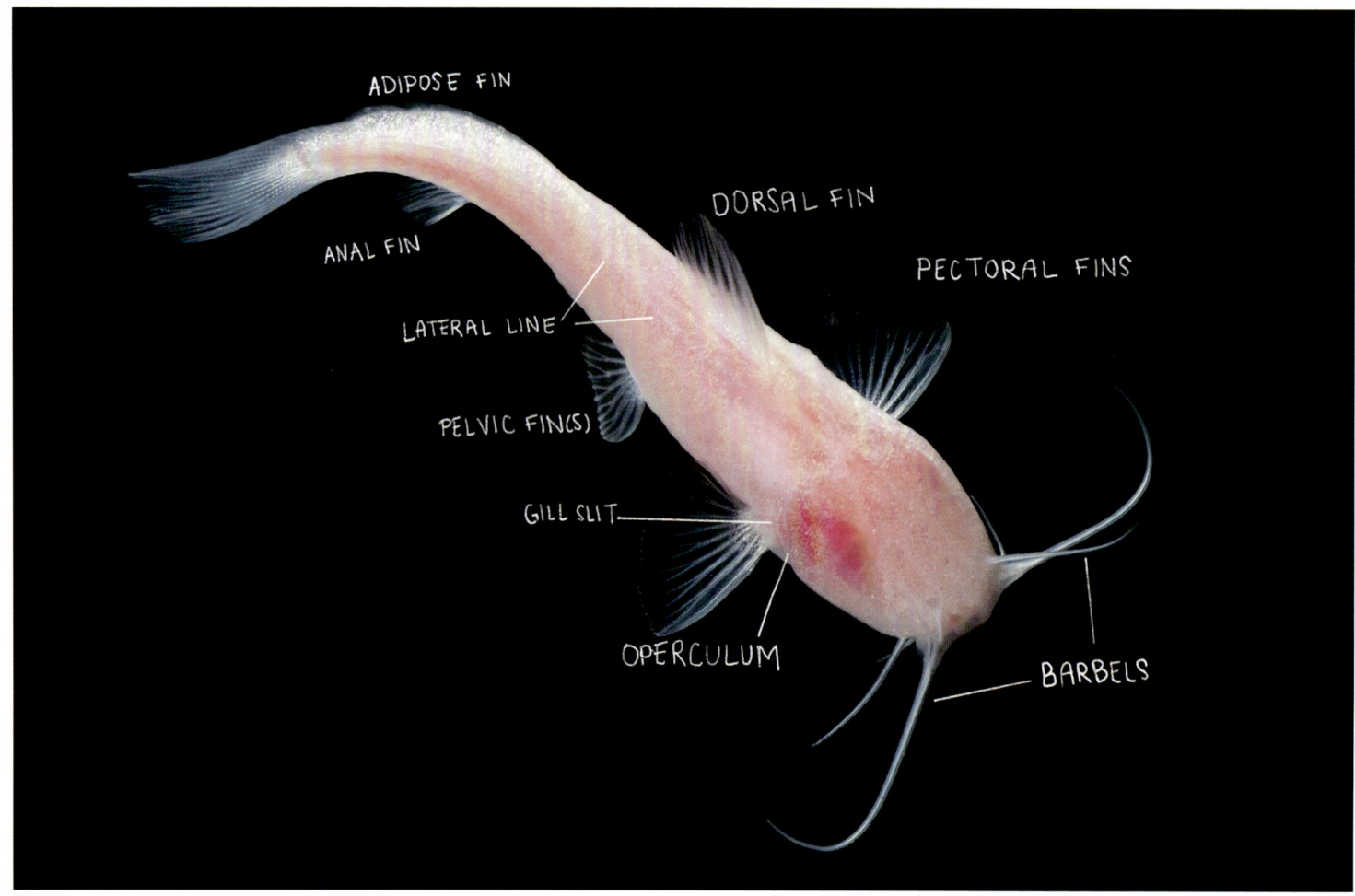

© Jean Krejca, Zara Environmental

When did the Species First Appear in Fossil Records?

The timeline on the facing page depicts the extraordinary length of time the Mexican blindcat has existed as a species.

Illustration by Campbell Lindstrom

Photograph by James May. The Mexican blindcat mural in Del Rio, Texas was painted by Roger Peet for the Center for Biological Diversity's Endangered Species Mural Project, in collaboration with the Casa De La Cultura in Del Rio.

Current and Future Research

If you are interested in learning more about the Mexican blindcat or other species in the aquifers of Texas and Mexico, the following groups provide up-to-date information:

Center for Conservation and Research at San Antonio Zoo

Blindcat Working Group

The Texas Speleological Survey

Edwards Aquifer Authority

Texas Parks and Wildlife Department

United States Fish and Wildlife Service

University of Texas at Austin Biodiversity Center

Texas Grotto Clubs

Center for Biological Diversity

Discussion Questions

How do you navigate in places that are unfamiliar? Have you ever had to rely on your other senses to navigate or figure something out? Synesthesia (sin-uh-stee-zhuh) is when an individual experiences one sense through another. For example, they might hear someone's name and see a particular color at the same time.

How did Blindcat and Tadpole experience synesthesia in the story?

How does the Mexican blindcat measure time? What is a "season"?

What special adaptations do blindcats have that allow them to live in a world with no light? How have they survived as a species for approximately thirty million years?

Blindcat's home is in an aquifer that spans two countries. What is the significance of the international border for the Mexican blindcat and other species who share resources?

What parts of the water cycle are described in this story?

What did you learn about Blindcat's ecosystem in the story?

Why is it important for us to keep our waterways clean? How can you help protect creeks, ponds, and aquifers from contamination?

Photo courtesy Jean Krejca, Zara Environmental

Notes from the Author

This story is fiction, but it is plausible that the events of this story could actually occur. I imagined the tale based on my time spent in nature at Lake Amistad and the San Felipe Springs and in Del Rio, Texas. After I wrote the story, I felt compelled to learn more about *Prietella phreatophila*. I spoke directly with scientists and conservation biologists. Information contained in the back of the book is factual.

One of the most helpful interviews I conducted was at the Center for Conservation and Research at the San Antonio Zoo where I was able to see the Mexican blindcat in person. It is the only facility in the world that houses the Mexican blindcat. The blindcat facility is not open to the public, but the zoo hopes to have them on display in the future.

The newest technology being used to search for blindcats is called environmental deoxyribonucleic acid (eDNA) sampling. Scientists collect water at a location, such as a private or public well, and separate the DNA using a membrane filter. The DNA can be frozen or preserved in a solution and brought to a laboratory for testing. In the laboratory, scientists detect DNA found in the sample and sequence its four bases adenine (A), guanine (G), cytosine (C), and thymine (T). Every living organism has a different pattern of bases, allowing scientists to detect which organisms are present in the water sample.

The Mexican blindcat is one of several blindcat species in the aquifers of Texas and Northern Mexico. Environmental DNA sampling has the potential to unveil more information about the aquifers and other blindcat species, such as the toothless blindcat, *Trogloglanis pattersoni*, or the widemouth blindcat, *Satan eurystomus*, both found in the Edwards Aquifer near San Antonio.

Photo courtesy Jean Krejca, Zara Environmental

Acknowledgments

This story never would have come to life without the support of my family and friends. My husband, Chris, has encouraged me to write from the very beginning. Lisa Nielsen, park ranger, teacher, and dear friend, imparted a lasting love of the natural flora and fauna of Del Rio, Texas. Ms. Margie Crisp, fellow TAMU Press author and naturalist, has been a wonderful mentor during the writing and publishing process.

Jessica and Jason Lindstrom along with their talented daughter, Campbell, helped me with childcare and the timeline illustration in the back of this book. Thank Jack Johnson and Nora Padilla of the National and State Park Service for exposing me to the beauty of our local landscape.

Peter Sprouse and his colleagues from Zara Environmental graciously shared information and photographs seen in this book. Mr. Sprouse put me in contact with Dr. Andy Gluesenkamp at the Center for Conservation and Research at the San Antonio Zoo. He introduced me to the real, live Mexican blindcat! Despite its tiny size, it is a brilliant creature. Dr. Andy's passion for conservation is contagious!

I would also like to thank Dr. Dean Hendrickson and his dedicated colleagues at the University of Texas at Austin Ichthyology Specimen Collection. Dr. Hendrickson is an expert on the Mexican blindcat. The visit to their lab gave me the chance to ask questions about the blindcat, its anatomy, and behavior. I even held a specimen of *Satan eurystomus*, a blindcat species that has not been seen alive for over fifty years in the aquifers of San Antonio!

Finally, a huge thank you to Bianka Santillan. Her love and dedication for this project exceeded my expectations. I am grateful she didn't think I was mad to write this story, and I am honored she agreed to work with me.

Photo courtesy Jean Krejca, Zara Environmental

Copyright © 2024 Lisa Johansson
All rights reserved
First edition

♾ This paper meets the requirements of ANSI/NISO Z39.48-1992
Binding materials have been chosen for durability.

Printed in China through Martin Book Management
Production Location: Shenzhen, China
Production Date: July, 2024
Cohort: Batch 1

Library of Congress Cataloging-in-Publication Data
Library of Congress Control Number: 2024941367
Identifiers: LCCN: 2024941367 | ISBN 9781648432507 (hardcover) | ISBN 9781648432514 (ebook)
LC record available at https://lccn.loc.gov/2024941367

Book design by Kristie Lee

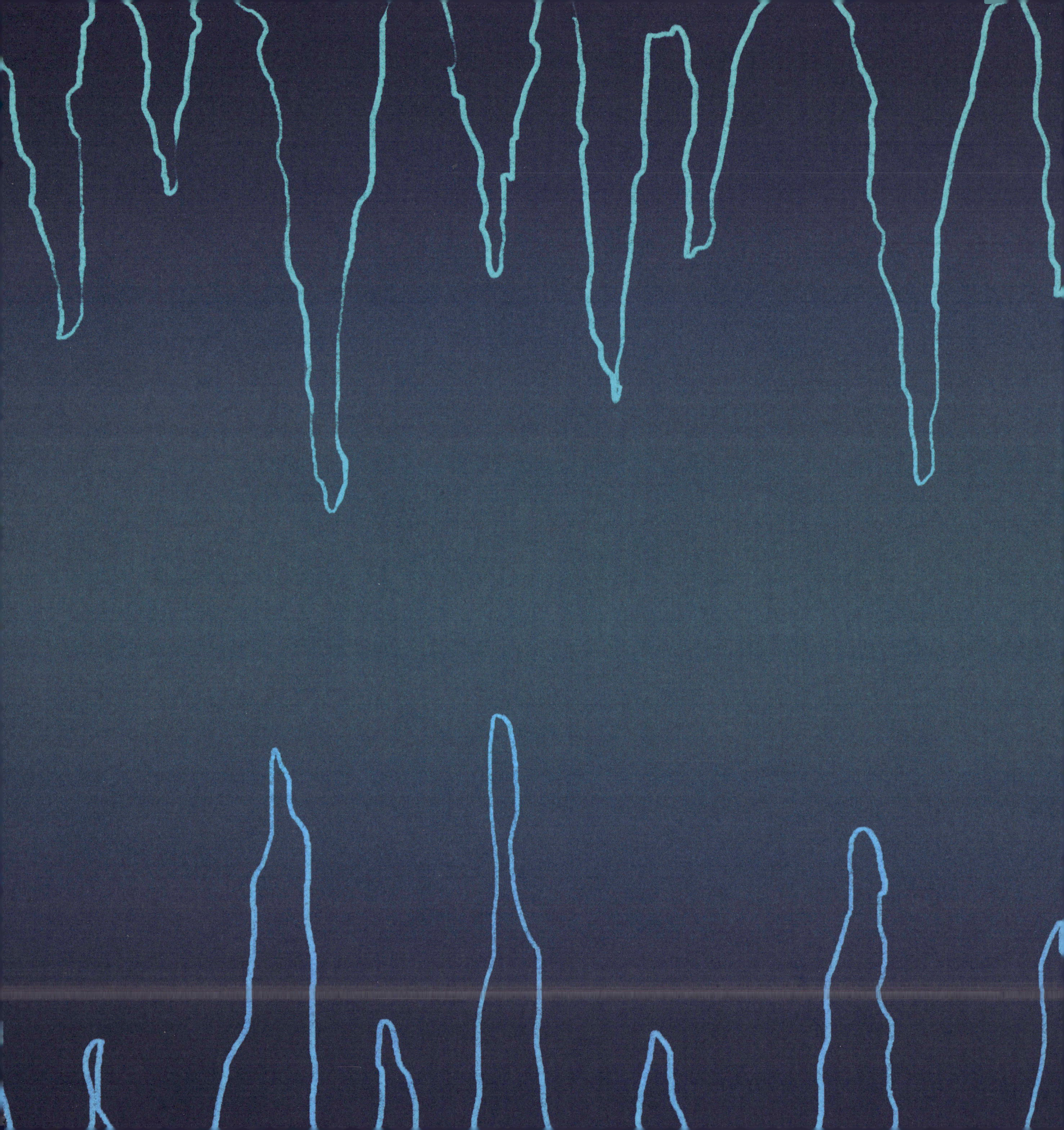